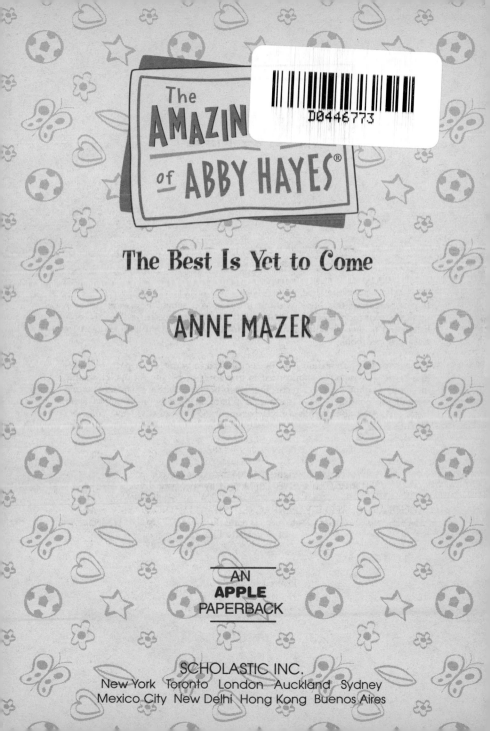

The AMAZING of ABBY HAYES®

The Best Is Yet to Come

ANNE MAZER

AN
APPLE
PAPERBACK

SCHOLASTIC INC.
New York Toronto London Auckland Sydney
Mexico City New Delhi Hong Kong Buenos Aires

To Joy
"The best is yet to come!"

No part of this publication may be reproduced in whole or in part, or stored in a retrieval system, or transmitted in any form or by any means, electronic, mechanical, photocopying, recording, or otherwise, without written permission of the publisher. For information regarding permission, write to Scholastic Inc., Attention: Permissions Department, 557 Broadway, New York, NY 10012.

ISBN 0-439-48282-8

Text copyright © 2004 by Anne Mazer.
All rights reserved. Published by Scholastic Inc.

SCHOLASTIC, APPLE PAPERBACKS, THE AMAZING DAYS OF ABBY HAYES, and associated logos are trademarks and/or registered trademarks of Scholastic Inc.

12 11 10 9 8 7   7 8 9/0

Printed in the U.S.A.   TK

First printing, June 2004

Chapter 1

Thursday

"The best is yet to come."

Sunshine and Blue Skies Calendar

YES! I hope this is true.

<u>Best of Best Things Yet to Come</u>

IN TWO WEEKS, I AM GRADUATING FROM FIFTH GRADE!

It seems like I've been in fifth grade forever! But I'm FINALLY going to sixth grade!!!

Hooray! Hooray! Hooray! Three cheers!
No, wait. That's not enough.
Three hundred cheers!

More Best Things Yet to Come

In the fall, I go to middle school.
I'm excited and a little scared.

Today at recess, my friend Hannah and
I had a conversation about it. We both
agreed that we'll like having a different
teacher for each class and meeting kids
from other parts of town.

I'm a little nervous because Susan B.
Anthony Middle School is so much bigger
than Lancaster Elementary. Our class visited
it last week. There are five different wings
and two levels in the middle school. The
cafeteria is the size of our gymnasium!

Hannah said not to worry, we'll figure it
out really fast. But our friend Mason told
us that his older sister, Kathleen, got lost on
her second day. She asked for help from an
eighth-grader, and he gave her the wrong di-
rections! Mason said that Kathleen's science
teacher got mad at her for showing up ten
minutes late, even though it wasn't her fault.

I hope this doesn't happen to me.

The person I'll miss most from Lancaster Elementary is Ms. Bunder. Her creative writing classes are the best!

Hannah's dad is a high school teacher. He says there are many fine teachers at Susan B. Anthony. But no one can ever replace Ms. Bunder.

Even though I'm scared and a little sad, I'm still really excited about sixth grade. Maybe I'll be a whole new person! I might make new friends, find new interests, and even have a new look. One more good thing about sixth grade: Hannah and I are a year closer to pierced ears!!! Our moms said we could get them pierced when we're in seventh grade.

Another Best Thing Yet to Come
The summer.

I have the entire summer ahead of me. It's going to be the best summer of my life!!! I just know it.

The Hayes family sat around the dining room table with glasses of iced tea and plates of strawberry-rhubarb pie in front of them.

"Great pie, Dad," fifteen-year-old Eva commented. She cut herself another slice.

"Thank you, Eva," Paul Hayes said with a smile.

"You're having *another* piece of pie?" her twin, Isabel, cried. "You already had a slice the size of Texas!"

"Since when are you the pie police?" Eva retorted.

Eight-year-old Alex made wailing siren noises. "They're coming to arrest you, Eva!"

"Have Mom defend you," Abby advised. "She's the best lawyer in town."

"None of my clients has ever gone to pie jail," Olivia said, holding up her hand. "I solemnly promise that Eva will be free to eat dessert forever more."

"We all have the inalienable right to liberty, justice, and the pursuit of pie," Paul Hayes added. He was a computer consultant, and he worked at home.

Isabel sighed dramatically. "This family is weird."

Eva helped herself to a large scoop of vanilla ice

cream. "Mmmm, delicious," she said to annoy her twin.

Under the table, Abby's cat, T-Jeff, meowed quietly. He rubbed his head against Abby's leg.

She reached down to scratch him behind the ears. "I bet you wish you were having pie and ice cream, too," she said to him.

"Don't even *think* about giving T-Jeff ice cream!" Isabel warned. "It'll make him sick!"

Abby and Isabel shared the care of T-Jeff. But Abby always secretly thought of him as *her* cat. She was the one who had hidden him in her room until her parents gave her permission to keep him.

"I wasn't going to," Abby protested. "I was just . . ."

Olivia clinked her spoon on a glass. "Our family meeting will now come to order!"

Everyone fell silent.

"Wow. How do you *do* that?" her husband murmured admiringly.

"Courtroom experience," Olivia replied. She banged her spoon again. "The Hayes family needs to discuss summer plans. You've all talked to your dad and me privately, but we want to hear everyone's plans again. This way, the whole family will get a sense of how the summer is going to work. We also need to coordinate rides."

Instantly, the dining room erupted into its usual chaos as all four of the Hayes siblings began to talk at once.

Olivia smiled at her husband.

"One at a time!" Paul said. "One at a time!"

"Me first!" Eva and Isabel both cried at once. "We're the oldest!"

"I'm the *youngest*," Alex protested.

"I'm the only one with red hair," Abby said. "Besides, no one *ever* starts in the middle."

"Good point," Paul said. He reached over and borrowed his wife's spoon to stir some sugar into his tea. "Tonight, Abby will go first. Tell everyone what you're doing, Abby."

Abby looked desperately around the room. "Well, I, uh, I . . . I didn't really expect to go first," she stammered.

Eva interrupted. "*I* have a job for the summer. I'll be an assistant coach at the youth sports camp. I'll be coaching girls' softball, swimming, basketball, and soccer." She leaned back in her chair with a pleased look on her face. "My day starts at seven-thirty and ends at five o'clock."

"Do you need a ride?" her father asked.

Eva shook her head. "I can ride the camp bus. I'll be home at six."

"That sounds great," said Paul.

"Abby?" Olivia said. "It's still your turn. Eva, you owe her an apology for interrupting."

"Sorry," Eva mumbled ungraciously.

"It's okay," Abby said. "I wasn't ready, anyway. And I'm still thinking about what to say."

"You'd never make it on any of *my* teams," Eva commented. "You need quick reflexes for all sports."

Isabel leaped to Abby's defense. "Didn't you hear her? She's *thinking*. Maybe you don't know what that is!"

Eva's face reddened. "I'm not stupid, Isabel! I'm in the Honor Society, just like you!"

"Girls . . ." Olivia sighed. She tapped her glass with the spoon again. "Alex, if Abby's not ready, it's your turn."

"I'm going to nature camp," Alex said. "We're studying bugs and learning to build shelters out of sticks and leaves!"

"I'll drive you in the morning," Olivia said, "and your father will pick you up in the afternoon. You need to make your own lunch."

Alex's eyes lit up. "How many cookies can I pack?"

"Three," Paul said firmly. "You'll make your own peanut butter and jelly sandwich, too. And don't forget napkins and a drink." He turned to Isabel. "Tell us your plans, Isabel."

"A playwriting workshop in the morning," Isabel announced, "and administrative work at the theater office in the afternoon. I don't need a ride," she added. "I'm riding my bike both ways."

"You need the exercise," Eva muttered.

Isabel ignored her. "I beat out one hundred applicants to get into the workshop," she said. "They only had ten spaces. It's a top-level program."

"We're very proud of you," Paul said.

"Yay, Isabel!" Alex cheered.

"Abby," Olivia said. "It's your turn. You've been very patient."

It wasn't hard to be patient when you didn't know what you were going to say. Abby had gotten her parents' approval for her summer plans. But it still made her nervous to announce them in front of her high-achieving, high-energy, highly scheduled siblings.

She reached down and petted T-Jeff. His purr made her feel more confident. "Well," she began. "I'm, um, not signed up for anything."

"You're doing *nothing?*" both Eva and Isabel cried.

In spite of their differences, her sisters were, at times, frighteningly similar.

"No camp?" Alex shouted. "You'll miss out on all the fun!"

Abby didn't respond. How could she explain her plans?

"Remember how you described it to your mother and me," Paul encouraged her.

"My plan is to have no plan," Abby began. "I don't want to go to camp this summer, and I'm not old enough to have a job. So I thought I could spend the summer going to the pool with my friends, playing with T-Jeff, reading, writing in my journal — you know, all the things I like to do . . ." Her voice trailed off.

She looked anxiously into her sisters' faces.

"What a good idea!" Isabel said. "Free time! Relaxation! *No one* does that anymore."

"It's especially good before sixth grade," Eva added. "Just wait. At Susan B. Anthony, there are so many activities and lots more homework. You'll never have this much free time again."

"Really?" Abby said.

Eva made a face. "Oh, yeah, you'll be busy every second of the day."

Abby looked worried.

Olivia shot Eva a warning look. "Abby is going to love sixth grade."

"I will," Abby agreed. "And I'm going to love my summer, too!"

Alex pouted. "I want a summer like Abby's."

"When you get older," his mother promised. She smiled at Abby. "Abby is mature enough to do this."

"I'll let you know where I am, who I'm with, what I'm doing, and when I'm coming home," Abby recited. "I'll make my own breakfast and lunch and clean up after myself. I won't interrupt Dad at work upstairs unless it's absolutely necessary." She took a breath. "I promise *never* to say, 'I'm bored.' "

"That's the most important pledge of all," Paul said. "You have to be responsible for scheduling your own time."

"But you need a *little* structure in your day,"

Olivia added. "Your father and I have decided that you need to sign up for one class or workshop. Maybe pottery classes, or sailing, or softball, or a book group at the library, or cooking class . . ."

T-Jeff jumped into Abby's lap and began to purr loudly.

"Sure," Abby agreed. "It sounds like fun. Why not?"

Chapter 2

Saturday three days
till
graduation!!!
"Beware of all enterprises
that require new clothes."
— Henry David Thoreau
The Emperor's New Calendar

Uh-oh. Today Hannah and I are going to the mall together. We have to buy new clothes for our fifth-grade moving-up ceremony. Our parents gave us money.

New clothes aren't exactly required, but most of the kids in our class will be wearing them.

Should we beware of our graduation?

Or should we wear old clothes instead?

But I don't have any old clothes to wear. I only have one dressy dress, and it's too small!

*   *   *

I also have to buy a new swimsuit, goggles, and earplugs. I am taking swimming lessons every morning at the city pool.

Should I beware of swimming lessons, too?

Swimming lessons weren't my first choice. But they were my only option.

There weren't any places left in the pottery class. I couldn't get into the writing circle at the library, the make-your-own-jewelry workshop, or the theater group. All of them filled up a month ago.

So I'm taking a swimming class.

At least I'll be in the pool. When I was younger, I took swimming lessons. They weren't too bad. I actually liked them a lot And swimming lessons are only an hour a day.

The rest of the time is MINE!

My other summer plans don't require new clothes. So I don't have to beware of petting the cat, writing in my journal, or hanging out with friends!!!

"Let's go in there," Hannah said, pointing to a store across the aisle in the mall.

"Pants Unlimited?" Abby said. "But we're supposed to be looking for *dresses*."

"I hate dresses," Hannah said. "Didn't you know that?"

"No," Abby said. "I just thought you never wore them."

She and Hannah had become friends a little less than a year ago when they met at a Fourth of July picnic. Hannah had accompanied Abby and her family on a camping trip a week later. Then Hannah's family had moved into Abby's neighborhood.

Now the two girls were practically best friends — especially since Jessy, Abby's former best friend, had moved to another state.

Hannah grabbed Abby's arm and steered her into the store. "My mother said I could wear pants if they were nice."

"You mean not jeans or cargo pants," Abby said.

"But maybe bell-bottoms, flares, capris, straight legs, slim cut, stretch, twill, baggy, overalls, shorts, skorts, or leggings," Hannah read from the

PANTS UNLIMITED sign. "They have every kind of pants in every color of the rainbow."

Abby gazed at the shelves and racks of pants. "It makes me dizzy to look at them all," she said. "How are we ever going to find what we need?"

"Over here," Hannah said. "See? It says DRESS PANTS."

The girls stood in front of a rack of silk, velvet, satin, and wool pants.

"What about these?" Abby said. She pointed to a pair of white silk pants embroidered with pale green flowers. "Only one hundred and thirty-five dollars."

"My mom would hit the roof," Hannah said. "She told me not to spend more than forty dollars on pants."

"These are ninety-five dollars," Abby said, checking out a pair of black satin pants. "And they're too sophisticated. They look like what Isabel or my mother might wear."

"Let's check out the sale rack," Hannah suggested. "Maybe we'll find something there."

The two girls made their way toward the back of the store.

"I can see why these are on sale." Abby pulled out a pair of fluorescent lime green capris.

"Abby! They're perfect!" Hannah joked. "Try them on!"

"No way," Abby said. "I am *not ever* wearing these pants. Not even in my dreams."

"I LOVE these!" Hannah suddenly cried. She held up a pair of orange silk pants. The cuffs were embroidered with polka dots. "Aren't they great?"

"Wow," Abby said. "They're so . . . orange!"

"They're so *me*!" Hannah cried delightedly. "And they're my size, too. I'm going to try them on."

"You're not serious," Abby said. "Would your mother let you wear them to the moving-up ceremony?"

"Why not?" Hannah said. "They're not jeans or cargos. What can anyone say against dressy orange silk pants?"

"Um, nothing, I guess," Abby said.

Unlike Abby, Hannah never seemed to worry about what people might think. She wasn't afraid to be herself.

Hannah took another pair from the rack. They were purple velvet, with a pink ribbon at the cuff. "Look! Here are the matching Abby pants. They're totally you!"

"I'm going to wear a dress," Abby said. She picked

up the pants and held them against her waist. "But these *are* really cute."

"Try them on," Hannah urged. She flipped over the price tag. "They were originally one hundred and twenty-five dollars. Now they're twenty-one."

Hannah glanced at the tag on the orange pants. "And these are fourteen dollars marked down from ninety-nine. Can you believe it? They're perfect, and bargains, too. Our mothers will be thrilled."

They found two empty dressing rooms next to each other. Abby slipped off her shoes and jeans. She pulled on the purple pants.

"How do yours look?" Abby called, zipping up the purple pants. "Mine fit okay. Actually, they look pretty good."

"Mine are incredible!" Hannah cried. "They were made for me."

The two girls emerged from their cubicles and stood in front of full-length mirrors.

"WOW!" Abby said when she saw Hannah in her orange pants. "Those *are* great! But I still can't see you wearing them to our graduation."

"*I* can," Hannah said. "With a hot pink ruffled blouse and orange flip-flops. It'll be so much fun."

Abby smiled at her friend. "No one will ever forget you."

"I think *you* should wear the purple pants to the moving-up ceremony," Hannah replied.

Abby surveyed herself critically in the mirror. She had to admit, the pants were flattering, and they were fun.

"I like them," Abby said slowly. "But I *was* planning to wear a dress."

"Everyone will be wearing dresses!" Hannah sighed. "Let's be different!"

"Well . . . maybe," Abby said.

Hannah flung her arms out wide. "We'll have the most dramatic and exciting outfits in the entire fifth grade!"

Chapter 3

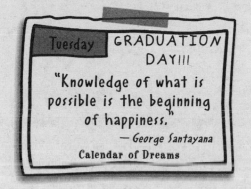

I know what is possible:

<u>EVERYTHING!!!</u>

1. Leaving Lancaster Elementary.
2. Moving up to sixth grade and going to Susan B. Anthony Middle School.
3. Becoming a new Abby Hayes.
4. Getting pierced ears (soon)!
5. Being more in charge of my life and my time.
6. Starting the BEST summer of my life.

* * *

If this is just the beginning of happiness, I'm going to burst!!

Question: Why do people burst from happiness? I feel more like I'm going to float or glide.

P.S. Hannah talked me into buying the purple velvet pants. She bought the orange silk pants. We're wearing them to the moving-up ceremony tonight.

P.P.S. I wasn't sure what my family would think about the pants, but they loved them.

Isabel said she wanted some just like them. Eva whistled. Mom said they were elegant and a great bargain. Dad said I looked cute!! Alex said I looked too grown-up. (I think that's a compliment.)

Mom helped me pick out a lime green blouse to wear with the pants. I also got matching green clogs.

WHEEE!!!!

P.P.P.S. Hannah is wearing a hot pink blouse with her orange pants. She is going to light up the gym. But her mother told her she couldn't wear orange flip-flops. She is wearing hot pink espadrilles instead.

P.P.P.P.S. I know that P.S. means "post-script," but wouldn't it be great if the P̲ meant "purple"?
Purple Purple Purple Purple Script!!!!

I LOVE purple!! I'm so glad that I'm wearing it to my fifth-grade graduation!!

"Purple Hayes," Ms. Bunder said to Abby. "That's who you are."

When Abby saw Ms. Bunder in the crowd of families and friends gathering for the ceremony in the school gym, she had rushed over to say good-bye to her favorite teacher.

"With a touch of green and pink," Abby added.

"You look wonderful!" Ms. Bunder said. "I'll always remember you like this."

"I'll miss you *so* much!" Abby cried. "You are the best teacher ever!"

"You'll have other good teachers," Ms. Bunder said. "Just don't stop writing, Abby."

"Okay, I won't," Abby promised. "I *couldn't* stop writing even if I wanted to."

"Spoken like a true writer," Ms. Bunder said with a smile. "I'll miss you, too. I hope you'll stay in touch. Let me know what you're writing."

"I will," Abby said.

Ms. Bunder handed her a small card with her address, phone number, and e-mail address. "This is where you can reach me."

"Thanks," Abby said. She was just about to tell Ms. Bunder that maybe they could be pen pals when Ms. Kantor and Mrs. McMillan, the two fifth-grade teachers, stepped up to the microphone.

"Will the fifth-graders please sit in the rows reserved for them," Ms. Kantor said. "And will everyone else have a seat. We want to start the ceremony in five minutes."

Ms. Bunder gave Abby a quick hug. "I'll be watching you!" she said.

Abby hurried toward the group of graduating students.

It was a hot June evening. The gym doors were open to let in a breeze. A few fans blew streams of warm air into the room.

Parents with digital cameras and camcorders crowded the aisles. Babies sat on their mothers' laps. Kids squirmed in the heat.

"Hey, Hayes," Casey said.

"Hi, Hoffman," Abby replied. It was their ritual greeting.

Casey was one of her closest friends. Sometimes kids teased Abby about her friendship with a boy, but Abby liked him too much to care.

Hannah joined them. As usual, she had a huge smile on her face.

"Wow!" Casey said, pointing to her bright orange pants. "Your mom let you wear those?"

"Aren't they great?" Hannah said enthusiastically.

Casey pointed to his dress shirt and slacks. "My mom *made* me wear these. She said I couldn't wear sweatpants and a T-shirt to my fifth-grade graduation."

"You look really different," Abby told him. "In a good way."

"We *all* do!" Hannah said.

The three friends glanced at their classmates. The

girls wore dresses or long skirts with fancy blouses. The boys wore button-down shirts and dress slacks. A few of them even had on ties.

Natalie, who normally showed up in sneakers and jeans, was almost unrecognizable in a long green skirt and a sleeveless top.

Bethany had on a short pale pink dress. Her hair was pinned up. She wore pink lipstick and a silver necklace.

"Bethany looks so much older," Casey started to say.

Suddenly, the crowd in front of the door parted. Brianna and her best friend, Victoria, made their entrance. Brianna was the best-dressed girl in fifth grade.

Tonight she was wearing a long white sheath dress. On her feet were high-heeled white sandals. She carried a small bouquet of flowers and smiled to the crowd as if they had gathered just for her.

"Does she think she's a bride?" someone muttered.

Victoria, the meanest girl in fifth grade, was right behind her. She wore a strapless red gown, and her hair was piled on her head in elaborate curls.

"It would have been funny if they had worn old jeans," Abby whispered to Hannah and Casey.

"Or really unfashionable clothes," Hannah whispered back. "That would have been hilarious."

"I don't think they have a sense of humor," Casey said.

"Like, we arrived in a limousine, you know," Victoria announced to the fifth-graders as she and Brianna made their way through the crowd like royalty. "It's going to, like, pick us up afterward and take us to this totally cool dance at the high school."

"My mother's cousin's girlfriend's uncle owns a limo service," Brianna bragged. "My father rented the limousine as a graduation gift. We have our own chauffeur."

"So do we," Abby said. "Our parents."

Casey started to laugh.

"It's so totally *not* the same!" Victoria snapped.

Brianna gestured to the families sitting in folding chairs. "I have thirty-seven relatives here tonight."

"My cousins, like, flew in from California," Victoria began. "They, like, chartered their own plane, you know . . ."

A loud burp announced the presence of Mason. The Big Burper was unusually neat. He wore a short-sleeved shirt tucked into slacks. His hair was slicked back. He even wore a red bow tie.

"That burp was a nine point five," Mason said with satisfaction. "I could be on TV."

Victoria's lip curled. "Do you have to be, like, so totally disgusting?" she said to Mason.

"Yes," Mason said. He looked as if he was about to say something ruder, but Ms. Kantor stepped up to the microphone and motioned for silence.

"Can everyone please sit down and be quiet?" she said. "We're ready to begin."

Chapter 4

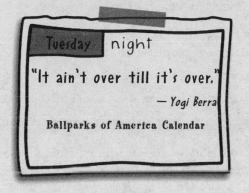

Tuesday night

"It ain't over till it's over."

— Yogi Berra

Ballparks of America Calendar

It's over!! Really, truly, absolutely, completely, utterly, without a doubt, sincerely, totally, entirely, and undeniably OVER.

I'm not a fifth-grader anymore!!!

HOORAY!!

Our graduation night was long. We had to stand in the hot gym and wait for our names to be called by our teachers.

Moving-Up Ceremony

1. Teacher calls student's name.
2. Student hurries to microphone.
3. Audience applauds.
4. Teacher says a few words about student, like "She worked very hard," or "He always had something funny to say."
5. Student shakes hands with teacher and principal, Ms. Yang.
6. Audience applauds again.

When Mason came to the microphone, there were whistles and shouts. Ms. Kantor said that she "expected the unexpected from Mason." (I thought he was going to answer with a world-class burp, but he smiled instead. Which proved that Ms. Kantor was right.)

Bethany was next. Ms. Kantor thanked her for sharing her love of animals with the class.

Then Hannah's name was called. Ms. Kantor said that Hannah's enthusiasm had lit up the classroom. "And your outfit is a perfect expression of it," she added with a smile.

Ms. Kantor didn't say anything about my outfit. (Purple is quieter than orange. Or maybe she didn't notice that I was wearing my favorite color.) Ms. Kantor said that she would always remember my love of writing.

Brianna was next. The yelling that greeted her was so wild that Ms. Kantor had to bang on the microphone ten times before she could speak.

When everyone finally quieted down, Ms. Kantor only said, "I don't know if I can add anything to that tribute."

What could anyone say about Brianna, anyway? She says it all herself!

But then Ms. Kantor said, "Brianna is unique," and everyone cheered wildly again. (I think someone should invent an applause o-meter for fifth-grade graduations.)

applause-o-meter

Brianna looked smug. She blew kisses to her "fans" and threw a flower into the crowd.

*   *   *

After a few minutes, Ms. Yang whispered in Brianna's ear that it was time to step down and let someone else graduate. If she hadn't, Brianna would have stayed there all night. We would have had the Fifth-Grade Graduation That Never Ended!

After every fifth-grade student had appeared, the chorus sang a song. Ms. Yang gave a short speech. Then it was over.

Hannah's dad gave both of us mortar-  boards, like they wear at college graduations. We tossed them in the air. Then we hugged our parents, joked with our friends, had punch and cake, and went home.

I AM NOW (ALMOST) A SIXTH-GRADER!

The summer has begun!!

Chapter 5

Friday

"Nothing is ours except time."

— *Seneca*

Wealth and Health Calendar

And I have ALL the time in the world to do everything I want!!! It's my perfect summer. My motto is "take things as they come."

I wake up to bright sunshine, not a loud alarm clock. (I don't even want to sleep late! I get up every morning at 6:30. It's almost unbelievable!)

I roll over in bed and write in my journal for half an hour. I don't rush downstairs to eat breakfast as fast as I can.

When I write, T-Jeff jumps on me and starts purring. When I'm happy, my cat's happy, too.

Then I get up, get dressed, have breakfast, and call Hannah. We decide what we're going to do for the day.

I do a few chores, like making my bed, feeding T-Jeff, and unloading the dishwasher.

My swimming lesson starts at 9:15 A.M. I walk to the city pool by myself. It's nice and cool in the morning. Sometimes I run into one of my friends along the way, and we talk for a few minutes.

I like the swimming lessons a lot.

The teacher is a college student named Jared. He's really friendly and nice. I got put into one of the more advanced swimming classes!!! I didn't know I was that good. Jared said I'm a natural swimmer.

Jared is the best instructor I've ever had. Maybe that's why my swimming is improving so quickly.

There are only three other kids in the class. Jared is teaching me how to improve my crawl and backstroke. He calls the crawl "freestyle." He's also teaching me the butterfly. (That's hard, but fun.)

I'm glad my parents made me take the swimming class. The only thing I don't like about it is that the water is usually COLD in the morning!

Jared says that it just means we have to swim harder and faster. His college swim team practiced outdoors in the fall at 6:00 A.M. The water was <u>really</u> cold!!

After my swimming lesson, I change in the locker room and walk home. Usually I have a snack in my gym bag, because swimming makes you hungry.

By the time I get home, it's only 10:30. I still have the whole day ahead of me!

Sometimes I meet Hannah and Casey at the park. We shoot hoops, ride our bikes, Rollerblade, and talk.

Later, we sit in my backyard and read under

the trees. Or we go to the pool to swim some more. (It's warmer in the afternoon.) Sometimes we go to the library or take Hannah's little sister, Elena, for a walk in her stroller.

Every day is magical.

Time is wonderful!

Especially when you can use it to do what you love.

"Wasn't that fun?" Hannah said as she and Abby made their way to the door of her house.

"Yes," Abby said. "I can't wait to do it again."

"Me, neither," Hannah replied. She held up her arm to show off the colorful bracelets she was wearing. "Thanks for the friendship bracelet, Abby. I love it!"

"Our two favorite colors, purple and orange," Abby commented. She pointed to the rainbow bracelet she was wearing. "I love the one you made for me, too."

The two girls had spent the afternoon making bracelets from a beading kit, sitting outside at a picnic table with boxes of beads, needles, and nylon thread. When they finished, they put the bracelets in small drawstring pouches — except for the ones they were wearing, of course.

"Let's try making necklaces next time," Hannah said. "Or earrings."

"I'm not buying or making any more earrings!" Abby cried. "Not until my mother lets me get my ears pierced."

"You'll be waiting until seventh grade, then," Hannah replied.

"We're almost sixth-graders now," Abby pointed out. "I can't wait another year. Our moms have to let us get our ears pierced *soon*."

"If your mom is like my mom, she won't *ever* change her mind," Hannah said.

"But I already have a drawerful of earrings," said Abby.

"You mean you have a secret collection?" Hannah asked eagerly.

"Sort of," Abby said. "I *think* my mother knows about it. But the rest of my family doesn't really."

"I'd like to see it someday," Hannah said.

"Sure," Abby agreed. She glanced at her watch. "I better get going. It's almost dinnertime."

Hannah opened the front door of her house. "Bye!" she called as Abby hurried down the stairs.

"See you tomorrow!"

* * *

As Abby walked into her house, T-Jeff bounded in front of her. Then he rubbed his head against her ankle.

"T-Jeff!" Abby said. "What have *you* been doing all day?"

She kneeled down to scratch her cat behind the ears. "Sorry I don't have a bracelet for you," Abby murmured. "Would you like a beaded cat collar?"

"Meow," T-Jeff said.

"I thought so," Abby answered.

"*There* you are, Abby," her father said with a smile. "Hurry up and wash your hands. We're about to eat dinner."

Abby gave T-Jeff one last pat on his head. "I'll be right there, Dad."

Olivia Hayes checked her watch. She was still wearing her work clothes — a tailored pale blue suit and a silk blouse. "You should have been home half an hour ago, Abby."

"Sorry, Mom," Abby said, sliding into her chair. She took the platter of chicken that Alex passed to her and put two pieces on her plate. "Hannah and I were making bracelets all afternoon. It was so much fun that I forgot all about the time."

Her mother took a drink of water. "I'm glad you had such a wonderful afternoon, but next time keep a better eye on the clock."

"I promise." Abby held up her arm to show off her rainbow bracelet. "See what Hannah made for me?"

"Beautiful!" her mother said. "Pass the green beans, Alex."

"It looks like a Hannah creation," Isabel commented. "Colorful and bright."

"We're going to make necklaces, too," Abby said.

"Next thing, you'll open a jewelry store in our house," her father teased.

"You can call it Beads 'n' Bangles," Eva said. "Or Ring-a-Ding."

Abby stuck out her tongue at her older sister.

"What did you do at camp today, Alex?" Olivia asked.

Alex put down his fork. "We learned about poison ivy," he said.

"I hope this wasn't a hands-on experience," Paul joked.

"We're itching to hear more," Eva said.

"One kid stepped right in the poison ivy," Alex announced. "With bare feet."

"Bare feet?" Isabel cried. "How could he be so stupid?"

Alex shrugged. "He had to go to the nurse's office."

Olivia's cell phone began to ring.

"We're eating dinner," Paul said. "Don't answer it."

"I *have* to. It might be important." With a grimace, Olivia fished the phone out of her suit jacket pocket. "Yes?" she said in a businesslike tone.

Suddenly, her face changed. "Laurie!" she cried. "Is it really you?"

"Laurie?" Paul Hayes said. "*Laurie?* Oh, boy."

"Certainly!" Olivia cried. "Laurie, you're always . . . yes, yes. Of course. Of course you can."

She stood up and paced around the dining room, murmuring into the cell phone. Abby and her sisters and brother stared at her. Their mother didn't usually interrupt dinner for personal calls.

Olivia clicked off the phone. "Guess who that was," she cried. "*Laurie!!* She's coming to visit on Sunday!"

"Who's Laurie?" asked Eva.

"Your mom's crazy friend from college," Paul said.

"She's not crazy," Olivia said. "She's *creative*."

Paul twirled his forefinger at his temple. "Cuckoo! Like a clock."

"Geniuses are often misunderstood," Olivia said firmly.

Paul almost choked on a green bean.

Abby, Isabel, Eva, and Alex glanced at one another.

Olivia ignored her husband. "You'll love Laurie," she said to her children. "In college, she started a band, Pink Plastic. She composed, sang, and played her own music."

"Wow," Eva said. "That sounds so cool. Is she famous?"

Olivia shook her head. "She never had the career she deserved."

"What is she doing now?" Isabel asked.

"I don't know," Olivia admitted. "That's the first phone call I've had from her in years. But I'm sure she's doing something creative and unusual."

Paul rolled his eyes. "She marches to the beat of a different drummer. Boom, boom."

"She's a *wonderful* person," Olivia said to her children. "You're going to love her."

Chapter 6

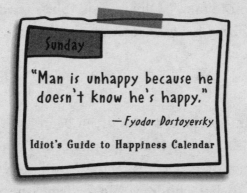

> **Sunday**
>
> "Man is unhappy because he doesn't know he's happy."
>
> — *Fyodor Dostoyevsky*
>
> **Idiot's Guide to Happiness Calendar**

Question: Why do quotes always say "man"? What about "woman," "boy," and "girl"?

If I wrote that quote, it would go like this:

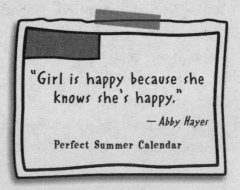

> "Girl is happy because she knows she's happy."
>
> — *Abby Hayes*
>
> **Perfect Summer Calendar**

I am happy AND I know it.

This is the best summer of my life. And now Mom's friend Laurie is coming to visit for a few days. Dad rolls his eyes every time her name is mentioned, but Mom says that Laurie is exciting, fun, and creative. She said it's never dull being around her.

I can't wait to meet Laurie. My summer will be even better once she arrives.

Abby placed clean towels on the newly made bed. A vase of flowers stood on a small bedside table, along with a few carefully chosen books. The windows were open, and a warm breeze blew into the guest room.

"What do you think?" Olivia asked. "Does the room need anything else?"

"It's perfect, Mom. Laurie will love it," Abby said.

Olivia gave Abby a quick hug. "I want her to be happy here." She paused. "I'll tell you a secret, Abby."

Abby's eyes widened. Her mother didn't confide in her very often.

"In college, Laurie was the star. She had better

grades, lots of boyfriends, and her own band. Every-one thought she was brilliant."

"But so are you!" Abby cried.

"Not really," Olivia said. "I've just worked really hard."

"Mom!" Abby protested.

"She was gorgeous," Olivia continued. "She was a dancer, too." She broke off suddenly. "I'm making lasagne for dinner, with a salad, and cherry cobbler for dessert. Lasagne is Laurie's favorite."

"I thought it was Dad's night to cook," Abby said in alarm. Her father was the main cook of the family. Olivia disliked cooking. When it was her night to make dinner, she ordered takeout.

"I *can* cook, Abby." Olivia got a stubborn look on her face. "I told your father I'd take charge of the meal tonight. I found a fabulous lasagne recipe with handmade noodles and three kinds of fresh cheeses. It's something you'd have to travel to Italy to find."

"It sounds like a lot of work," Abby said doubt-fully.

"I can handle it," her mother said.

Later that afternoon, Abby tiptoed through the kitchen.

It had been turned upside down. There were canisters of flour, sugar, and noodles on the counters. Bottles of olive oil and bowls of grated cheese stood amid overflowing cups of milk and sticks of butter. There were colanders of vegetables and bags of lettuce.

In the midst of the chaos, Olivia Hayes was pitting cherries. Her nose had a streak of flour across its tip. Her apron was stained with oil and juice. Her hair was falling across her face.

"What?" she asked irritably.

"I'm getting a glass of juice," Abby explained. She poured herself some orange juice and added seltzer and ice.

"Are you, Eva, Isabel, and Alex doing your jobs? Is the house clean and picked up?" Olivia demanded.

"It's so clean that it doesn't even look like our house anymore." Abby tactfully didn't include the kitchen.

"*Good,*" her mother answered.

"It smells great in here," Abby said.

"Does it?" her mother said. "It must be the lasagne baking." Olivia glanced at the clock and frowned. "I hope I have time to take a shower." She piled cherries into a bowl.

"I must have been mad to make cherry cobbler," she muttered. "Pitting *every single cherry*! It takes *years*."

Alex clomped into the kitchen. "I'm setting the table *now*," he announced. He took out a stack of plates and piled paper napkins on top of them. "And then I'm going to play computer games."

"Use *cloth* napkins, Alex, and our nice blue plates, not the chipped ones," his mother said. "Get out the silver. And be sure to change out of those filthy pants before Laurie gets here."

"Is she the president or something?" Alex grumbled.

"Mom, your face looks like a modern painting." Isabel came into the kitchen carrying a load of dirty laundry. "With lots of dots and streaks."

Her mother frowned and rubbed at her cheek. "Is that better?"

"You still have flour on your nose," Isabel said. "And a smear of cherry juice on your forehead."

Olivia sighed. "In fifteen minutes, the cobbler will be in the oven, and I'll clean up everything, including me."

The doorbell rang.

"That's *not* her," Olivia said. "It's just too early."

"Abby, get it," Isabel ordered. "You're the only one who's not doing anything."

"I've been working all afternoon!" Abby started to protest, but then she saw her mother's face.

"Never mind." Abby put down her drink. "I'll get it. It's probably Hannah, anyway. She said she might stop by."

Chapter 7

Sunday

"Timing is everything."
Boiled Egg Calendar

Yeah.

When I opened the door, I didn't see Hannah. A woman and a little girl were standing there.

The woman looked like an ordinary mother. She wore jeans and a baggy T-shirt with a picture of a dolphin on it. There was a backpack on her shoulders.

The little girl was about five. Her hair was in two messy braids. She was wearing jeans and a dirty yellow T-shirt. She didn't look happy to be on our porch.

I guessed that they were selling chocolate bars or magazine subscriptions for a peewee softball team.

"We're not buying," I said quickly. "Sorry."

I knew it wasn't a good time to ask my parents for money. It wasn't a good time to ask my parents for <u>anything</u>.

The woman raised her eyebrows. "We're not selling," she answered.

The little girl stared at me.

"I'm here to see Olivia Hayes," the woman said. "Is this her house?"

"Are you . . ." I stopped. The woman in front of me didn't seem anything like the fabulous person my mother had described. She didn't look intelligent, gorgeous, or talented. Or even particularly friendly.

"I'm Laurie," Laurie said.

"You are?" For a moment I didn't believe her. She didn't have any suitcases, and she wasn't alone. Plus, it was kind of early.

"You <u>are</u> expecting me, right?" Laurie asked.

I nodded. My face felt as hot as a furnace. It was probably cherry red.

"This is my daughter, Wynter," she said.

The little girl stuck one of her braids into her mouth and chewed on it.

"Winter?" I repeated. "Like the season?"

"Wynter," Laurie said, "with a y."

I invited them into the house and ran to get Mom. She had just put the cobbler in the oven.

"It's her!" I hissed. "Laurie! And she has a little girl with her!"

"A little girl?" Mom looked flustered. "She has a daughter?"

"Her name is Wynter," I said. "With a y. You know, like Summer. Or Spryng."

Mom didn't laugh. "I don't have a bed made up for her. She'll have to sleep on the floor of the guest room." She ran floury fingers through her hair. "Where are they now?"

"The front hallway," I said.

Mom groaned. "I can't believe she's here already."

*   *   *

If timing is everything, Laurie's was the WORST ever! She was two hours early.

And no one knew she was bringing a daughter. No one knew she even HAD a daughter.

She will get a mention in the Hayes Book of World Records for Most Untimely Arrival and Most Startling Memory Lapse. (How could she forget to tell Mom about her daughter?)

I will get a mention for Most Awkward Welcome. I hope Laurie doesn't mention that I mistook her for a candy bar saleswoman.

Olivia Hayes will receive a citation in the Hayes Book of World Records for Fastest Quick-Change in Hayes History. When she heard that Laurie was really here, she disappeared up the back stairs and reappeared in what seemed like two minutes.

Before: Stained, rumpled clothing. Smears of food on face and clothes. Messy hair. Unhappy, overwhelmed look.

<u>After:</u> Tailored pants and elegant shirt. Hair combed and in bun. Makeup. Leather sandals. She looked WAY better than Laurie did.

My mother cast one despairing look around the messy, disorganized kitchen, glanced at her freshly made-up face in the mirror, then hurried out to meet the guests.

The <u>Hayes Book of World Records</u> is also giving special awards to the Hayes siblings. (That's US!) While our mother was seeing her friend for the first time in fifteen years, we cleaned up the kitchen.

Eva and Isabel got the cobbler and the lasagne out of the oven at just the right moments. Eva made garlic bread. Isabel got out the drinks. Alex and I made salad and set a place for Wynter at the table. Isabel lit candles. And we didn't have a single argument!!

Then we went into the living room to tell everyone it was time for dinner.

Chapter 8

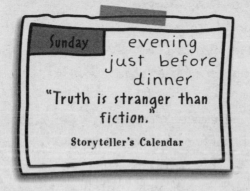

The following is a TRUE transcript of a TRUE conversation. It really and TRULY happened. (Trust me.) Truth is very strange!!!

As we all went into the living room to get Mom, Laurie, and Wynter, Dad came down from his home office.

He had changed out of his T-shirt into a pale green button-down shirt. His hair was combed, and he was wearing aftershave. He greeted Laurie with a friendly smile.

"You remember Paul, don't you?" Mom said to Laurie.

Laurie stuck out her hand. "Hey," she said. "The family man."

"It's good to see you again," Dad replied. He glanced at Wynter. "Is this your daughter?" he said. "What a cute girl."

"Cute?" Laurie repeated. "We don't use that word. It gives Wynter the message that she's only valued for her looks."

"I'm sure she's very intelligent," Dad said. "It was intended as a compliment."

Wynter stuck her braid in her mouth.

"No one condescends to girls in this house, Laurie," my mother said. "I have three wonderful daughters. And a wonderful son, too," she added.

"I'm extremely wonderful," Alex said.

I stuck out my tongue at him.

"Stop bragging," Isabel ordered him. "Pip-squeak."

"Where's the bathroom?" Laurie asked suddenly. "Wynter, you haven't gone in two and a half hours."

Wynter shook her head furiously.

"Are you sure, Wynter? You know what

happens when you hold it in. You need to
go to the bathroom now. Remember how we
discussed this on the way over here?"

"No," Wynter said. "It's my choice."

"You're right. It's your choice to wet
your pants or not," Laurie agreed.

I would write more about this FASCI-
NATING and TRUE conversation, but I
have to end this journal entry now.

"Are you still singing with Pink Plastic?" Olivia
asked Laurie. Her eyes shone with admiration. "You
were the best."

"Good heavens, no," Laurie said. "Pink Plastic
ended *years* ago. I'm out on my own now. I've toured
all over the U.S. and Canada. I have fans everywhere."

"Do you have a fan club?" Isabel asked.

"Mm-hmm," Laurie said. "And now I have an incredible career-making opportunity."

"Really?" Olivia said.

"Let's sit down to dinner, everyone," Paul Hayes
interrupted. "Laurie and Wynter must be hungry after their long drive. Olivia has spent the afternoon

making a delicious dinner in your honor," he said to Laurie.

"You cook, Livy?" Laurie said in disbelief. "In college you couldn't boil an egg."

"Olivia is a great cook! She makes incredible gourmet meals," Paul lied.

The other members of the Hayes family remained tactfully silent.

Paul continued. "*And* she's a partner in a major law firm in town."

"Livy?" Laurie said. "Not possible."

"Mom's the greatest!" Alex cried.

Olivia smiled. "Paul, will you escort Laurie into the dining room? Abby, you can show Wynter her place."

Abby held out her hand to Wynter.

Wynter jerked away.

"Okay, just follow me," Abby said. "I'll show you where to sit." She wondered if she should put a plastic sheet or a folded-up towel on Wynter's chair first.

"I don't like salad, Laurie," Wynter said. They were the first words she'd spoken since the family sat down for dinner.

"You don't like salad?" Isabel repeated. "But this

one is special. It was made by hundreds of salad trees all over the world just for you."

Eva speared a large piece of lettuce on her fork. "Mmmm, delicious. It's so fresh and crisp."

Wynter stared at the twins as if they were crazy.

"Want a piece?" Eva offered. She held out her fork. "It's *really* good."

"Taste it," Isabel urged.

"It's your choice, Wynter." Laurie turned to the rest of the Hayes family. "Her father and I are bringing her up to think for herself," she explained. "Derek and I aren't together anymore, but Wynter spends a lot of time with him."

"Oh," Paul Hayes said.

The Hayes siblings exchanged silent glances.

"It's your choice to eat salad or not," Laurie said again to Wynter. "Think it over carefully."

Wynter stuck a braid in her mouth.

"It's your choice to eat braids or not," Eva muttered under her breath. "Think it over carefully."

Abby looked down at her lap, trying to keep a straight face.

Laurie unfolded her napkin. "Anyway, as I was telling you, Livy, I've been on my own for the last ten years. I've played in Boston, Seattle, and New York.

And now I'm on the threshold of international success."

"*International* success?" Olivia gazed wide-eyed at her old college friend.

"Paris, London, Milan, Frankfurt," Laurie said. "A European tour. In the fall."

"Laurie!" Wynter said.

"Yes, Wynter?"

"My stomach hurts. I want to lie down."

"Okay, if that's your choice," Laurie said.

"Do you need to use the bathroom?" Isabel asked Wynter. "I'll show you where it is."

"No!" Wynter insisted. She got out of her chair and lay down on the floor.

There was an awkward silence.

Paul got up and pushed back his chair. "Ready for the main course?" he asked in a hearty voice. "I'll bring it out now."

"I'll help." Isabel stepped over Wynter's prone body and hurried after her father.

"I'm eating dinner on the floor," Wynter announced. "Without a fork."

Laurie nodded.

* * *

Paul carried in a tray of hot lasagne. Isabel followed with garlic bread and freshly grated Parmesan cheese.

"Your favorites, Laurie," Olivia said, with a fond glance. "We even have cherry cobbler for dessert."

"She hand-pitted the cherries," Paul boasted. "It took hours. But wait until you taste it!"

"We don't eat wheat, sugar, or dairy," Laurie said bluntly.

Olivia's face fell. "Why didn't you tell me? I would have roasted a chicken."

"We don't eat meat, either," Laurie said. "Unless it's free-range and organic."

"Then there's nothing here for you and Wynter. Except salad," said Olivia.

"I hate salad," Wynter said.

"I brought my own supplies." Laurie took several zipped plastic bags out of her backpack. She tossed one onto the floor next to Wynter. "Nuts and seeds. Carob chips. Dried fruit. Sesame spelt crackers."

Paul took a large piece of lasagne. "I'm going to enjoy every bite," he announced. "I think Olivia has outdone herself."

"It looks great, Mom," Abby echoed.

"Lasagne clogs the arteries," Laurie said, taking a

handful of small gray seeds from her plastic bag. "Your intestines have to work extra hard to get rid of all the fats, poisons, and toxins."

"Pass the poison, please," Eva muttered under her breath to Isabel.

"I don't like this!" Wynter spat out a mouthful of chewed-up seeds and dried fruit. It landed on the rug.

"Don't spit at the dinner table, Wynter," Laurie said.

"I'm not at the dinner table," Wynter announced. "I'm on the floor."

"Garlic bread, anyone?" Isabel asked sweetly.

"Thank you, Isabel," Olivia said, breaking off a piece and putting it on her plate. She glanced at Wynter. "Would you like a glass of grape juice?"

"She only drinks freshly squeezed juices of fruits grown without chemicals or pesticides," Laurie warned.

On the floor, Wynter made more spitting noises.

"Delicious lasagne, honey," Paul said.

"I hope your cholesterol is low," Laurie remarked. "That's heart-attack material."

"Can we change the subject?" Paul said. "This conversation is not good for my health."

"Amen," Isabel muttered.

Olivia turned to Laurie. "Remember that huge

party our dorm had the night before graduation?" she asked. "Pink Plastic played until the next morning. No one would let you stop. You were brilliant."

"All-night parties, Mom?" Eva said.

Laurie popped another handful of seeds into her mouth. "All I remember is how shy Olivia was. She kept to herself all night, too scared to say a word to anyone."

"I was?" Olivia said.

"That doesn't sound like Mom," Abby said. "I mean, she hosts dinners and entertains clients all the time."

"She wasn't like that in college. She was a real wallflower. Most of the time, people didn't know she was in the room." Laurie gave a little laugh. "I'd never have imagined you turning out like this, Livy. You're so *suburban*!"

"We've all changed," Olivia said. "Don't you think having children and a responsible job turns you into a whole new person?"

"*I've* hung on to my ideals," Laurie said.

"What are you saying?" Olivia said with a frown.

Laurie spilled a small pile of dried fruits onto her empty plate. "Oh, nothing," she said.

There was a short, awkward silence.

"So, Laurie, what brings you to town?" Paul said. "A sudden urge to see an old college friend, or is there something else going on?"

"I have a gig Thursday night. I'm still a musician, just like I was in college."

"That's wonderful," Olivia said. "Where are you playing?"

"At the Driftwood," said Laurie.

"How much are the tickets?" Olivia asked. "We'll all come."

"The tickets are on me," Laurie said. "I'm treating the Hayes family."

"Isn't this fantastic, everyone?" Olivia cried. "A real musician is staying at our house! And we'll be special guests at her show."

Laurie smiled smugly. "You knew me before I was famous." She rummaged in her backpack and pulled out a carton of carob-flavored soy milk.

Alex kicked Abby under the table. Eva and Isabel exchanged glances.

Paul sighed deeply. He pushed back his chair and began to clear the table.

Chapter 9

Tuesday

"The oldest friendships
ought to be the most
delightful."

— Cicero

Best Friend Calendar

Maybe Mom and Laurie's friendship is delightful to THEM, but it isn't delightful for the rest of us!

Laurie has been here for two days now. All she does is talk about herself and her career — and tell Wynter about her "choices." The word "choice" has become the least favorite word of the entire Hayes family! Well, almost the entire family. We're also sick of their weird habits, like Wynter calling Laurie by her first name. And their weird diet. Laurie is like a hamster. She

nibbles on nuts and seeds all day long. She won't eat the food we serve.

Mom acts like Laurie is the sun, the moon, and the stars. Everything revolves around Laurie. Laurie is THE most important person in the world. She and Laurie go to her room and have long private talks together. Whatever Laurie wants, Laurie gets. Mom doesn't seem to notice how awful she is.

Dad calls her Loony Laurie behind her back. If he sees her coming, he disappears into his office.

Eva, Alex, and Isabel are not home most of the time. But they can't stand Laurie and Wynter, either.

Thank goodness I still have my wonderful summer. At least during the day.

Every morning I leave early for the pool. I love the lessons with Jared! When I'm done, I go to Han-

nah's house. I don't return home until supper time. I put it off as long as I can.

Abby emerged from underwater and climbed up the
ladder at the side of the pool.

"That's it!" Jared said. "You did half a mile."

Abby pulled off her swim cap and ran her hands
through her wet curly hair. "Half a mile? Wait until I
tell my friend Hannah!"

"Your strokes are improving a lot," Jared said
"And so are your times. Now that you're a sixth-
grader, you can join the swim team this fall."

"Really?" Abby grabbed her towel and wrapped it
around her shoulders. "Do you think I can do it?"

"Of course you can. You're a natural. You
were born to be a swimmer! It's a lot of work, though,"
he warned. "You'll swim a couple of hours a day."

"I'll be really strong and healthy." Abby tried to
imagine herself swimming two hours a day. Maybe
she'd swim faster than Eva.

Abby smiled at the thought of beating Eva at *any*
sport. It would be like getting higher honors than
Isabel.

"It's the best exercise," Jared said. "And a lifelong
sport."

"Okay, I'll think about it." Abby slipped her feet into sandals and picked up her swim bag. "Maybe Hannah will join, too. I'll ask her today."

At 5:15 P.M., Abby opened the front door of her house.

"I'm home!" she yelled. "We had *fun*!"

After her swim lesson, Abby had gone straight to Hannah's house. Hannah's mother, Susan, had taken Abby and Hannah to a state park. The girls went swimming under a waterfall and picnicked with Susan and Elena. Then they hiked on a beautiful trail. It had been a perfect day.

Hannah loved the idea of joining a swim team with Abby. Susan thought it was a great idea, too.

Now Abby put down her swim bag and glanced at her reflection in the hall mirror. Her face was tanned. Her hair was even curlier and messier than usual. With a satisfied sigh, she adjusted the strap of her tank top and walked into the kitchen.

"There you are, Abby," her father said. He was chopping onions and tomatoes. "I'm making pasta with homemade tomato sauce for supper."

"Isn't that wheat?" Abby said. In the past two days, she and the other members of the Hayes family had become unwilling experts in which foods contained wheat, fats, and sugars.

Paul winked at her. "Guess what? The linguine is made from artichokes."

"*Artichoke* linguine? Do we have to eat it?" Abby cried.

"I'm also making a pot of regular spaghetti."

"Dad, you're the best!"

Her father sighed. "I hope this visit is over soon."

"Me, too!" Abby said.

"I'm counting the minutes," Paul said, putting the chopped onions in a frying pan. "Will you put away the clean dishes in the dishwasher?"

"Sure, Dad." Abby opened a cupboard and began to stack plates.

"How was your swimming lesson?" Paul asked. "Did you have fun with Hannah?"

"Nothing can ruin my summer, Dad, not even — " Abby began.

The back door swung open. Olivia entered the kitchen with bags of groceries in her arms, followed by Laurie and Wynter.

"A husband in the kitchen," Laurie said with a snicker. "That's where they belong."

"Hello, Laurie." Paul Hayes gave a tomato an

extra-hard chop. "I hope you bought garlic and peppers," he said to his wife.

"Right in this bag." Olivia deposited it on the counter next to her husband. She gave him a kiss and then began to unload the groceries.

Abby peered into one of the bags. It was stuffed with seeds, nuts, and dried fruits as well as soy milk, rice crackers, and unsweetened almond butter. "Mom, you went to the health-food store?" she asked.

"Laurie and Wynter are our guests," Olivia explained. "And this is what they eat. I'd like to show them some real Hayes hospitality."

"The lady of the manor speaks." Laurie plopped herself down in a kitchen chair and fanned herself with a catalog. "I hope you're not making wheat pasta," she said to Paul.

"Have no fear, artichoke pasta is here," Paul said lightly. "With Paul's special sauce, made from scratch."

Wynter wiped dirty hands on her stained yellow T-shirt. "I hate sauce."

"My homemade tomato sauce is served only in the finest restaurants," Paul said in a bad French accent. "It's beloved by children and adults around the world."

Neither Laurie nor Wynter smiled.

Abby searched through the bags. "Mom, where's my Tooty Frooty cereal? I wrote it on the list."

"Tooty Frooty has dozens of artificial colors, flavors, and sweeteners," Laurie said. "You're eating a bowl of chemicals every morning."

"I bought you some papaya peanut granola, Abby," Olivia said a bit defensively. "Laurie told me it's delicious."

"Mom! I *love* Tooty Frooty!" Abby cried.

Laurie opened a bag of roasted soy nuts. "Have you ever tried these, Abby? They're very good for you."

Abby didn't reply. She pulled the silverware drawer open and began putting away forks and knives.

"Come up to my office after supper," her father whispered. "I'll share my chocolate stash with you."

"What did you say?" Olivia asked.

"I just told Abby that soy nuts are full of protein," Paul said with a straight face.

"Now she can make an informed choice without being brainwashed by television," Laurie said approvingly.

"I'm *not* brainwashed," Abby muttered.

Laurie glanced at the clock. "Can I leave Wynter

with one of you tomorrow? I have a meeting and a rehearsal for my show."

"I'm working on a deadline," Paul Hayes said quickly. "So I can't help you out."

"Same here," Olivia said apologetically. "I'm in court all day."

"What about one of the girls?" Laurie asked. "Eva or Isabel?"

"They can't take Wynter," Olivia said. She put a container of goat milk in the refrigerator. "They're booked solid."

Abby hung up a frying pan and a pot over the stove. She hoped she was too young to watch Wynter. Or too curly-haired. Or too full of artificially flavored and colored Tooty Frooty.

Laurie gave her a long, appraising look. "What about *you*, Abby?"

"She's old enough," Olivia said. "And she's not overscheduled like the rest of us."

"Well, I'm doing, um, stuff with Hannah tomorrow, but, uh, I . . ."

"You and Hannah can include Wynter in your plans," Olivia said firmly. "Maybe you can take her to the park or the zoo."

"Abby!" Wynter pulled her braid out of her mouth. "I want to play with you and your friend."

"Is that your choice, Wynter?" Laurie said.

Wynter nodded and stuck the braid back in her mouth.

"Wonderful," Olivia said, as if everything were settled. "Come straight home after your swimming lesson, Abby. You see, Laurie, we *can* get things right around here."

"The perfect little suburban family," Laurie said lightly. "I'll leave as soon as Abby is home from swimming."

"But . . ." Abby's voice trailed off. This had all happened too fast. What about her plans for the day? Why did everyone *else* have a choice, but she didn't?

She looked toward her father for support. But for once, he had nothing to say.

Chapter 10

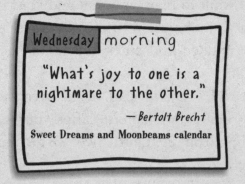

Wednesday morning

"What's joy to one is a nightmare to the other."

— *Bertolt Brecht*

Sweet Dreams and Moonbeams calendar

<u>Fact:</u> Wynter and I are spending the day together.

<u>Fact:</u> This is a joy to Wynter.

<u>Fact:</u> My mother and Laurie are also very happy.

<u>Fact:</u> Everyone is overjoyed, except me! I'm having a nightmare!

Did I get this responsibility because I am the only unoverscheduled person in the Hayes family? Is this some kind of happiness tax?

Nine Reasons I Don't Want to
Watch Wynter (A Partial List)

1. She whines. (All the time!)
2. She chews her braid. (Is hair organic?)
3. She wears the same yellow T-shirt every day. (It looks like a dirty tablecloth.)
4. She wipes her hands on her clothes. (Because we don't have unbleached napkins?)
5. She teases T-Jeff. (He hides under the couch when he sees her.)

6. She doesn't take baths. (It's her choice.)
7. She gets her own way ALL the time
8. She calls her mother by her first name. (Ugh!)
9. Laurie didn't even say please or thank you. She acts like she's doing ME a favor.

Eva and Isabel both told me I should have had a say in whether I wanted to babysit Wynter.

They also seemed relieved that they didn't have to do it.

Alex locks his room whenever Wynter is around. He says she breaks his robots.

Last night I called Hannah and told her the news.

"Mom said we had to include Wynter in our plans," I said glumly. "But you don't have to spend the day with us. I can watch Wynter on my own."

"I'll be there," Hannah said.

"Are you sure?" I asked her.

"I love a challenge," Hannah said. "Besides, it's just one day."

"It's gonna be a LONG one!" I cried.

But Hannah insisted on coming along.

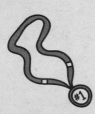

I will give her an award in the <u>Hayes Book of World Records</u> for Fabulous, Fearless, and Faithful Friendship.

Chapter 11

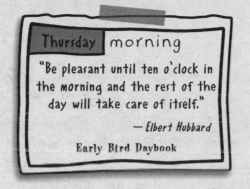

Thursday morning

"Be pleasant until ten o'clock in the morning and the rest of the day will take care of itself."

— *Elbert Hubbard*

Early Bird Daybook

Oh, yeah?

It was easy to be pleasant until ten o'clock in the morning yesterday. All I had to do was eat breakfast, get dressed, and walk to the pool for my swimming lesson.

Jared taught me the dolphin kick. He said I did it really well for my first time.

"What do I keep telling you? You're a natural," he said.

I wanted to stay in the pool forever.

But I couldn't. I got out and dried myself off.

And then I walked home.

Why It Became Harder to Be Pleasant

1. Wynter was waiting for me on the
front steps of my house.

2. She was wearing her ratty, filthy
clothes.

3. She was chewing on what was left of
her braid.

4. She whined, "Laurie wants to see
you."

Why It Became Extremely Difficult to Be Pleasant (But I Managed Anyway and I Ought to Win a Prize)

1. Laurie greeted me with, "There you are.
Finally. I have to leave in five minutes."

2. She gave me rapid-fire instructions:
"Remind her to go to the bathroom. There
are dry pants in her backpack if she has
an accident. Put sunscreen on her if you're
out in the sun. Don't let her wander off.

Make sure she doesn't get pushed around by bullies. She's so sensitive. Give her a healthy lunch. No fats, sweets, meats, or wheats. And make sure she always has a <u>choice</u>."

3. Her final words were: "Livy says you're very responsible. I guess you don't take after her."

Then she laughed, to make it seem like a joke, hugged Wynter, and rushed out of the house.

I was giving up my whole day to watch Wynter. And Laurie had insulted my mother!

Considering the situation, I was UNBE-LIEVABLY pleasant. How come the rest of the day didn't take care of itself?

<u>Hannah and Abby's Disastrous Day with Wynter in</u> the <u>Summer</u>
<u>Part One.</u> Hannah and I took her to the zoo. We wanted to see the monkeys, but Wynter said they

were stupid and sat down on the ground. She refused to budge until we bought her a large pink cotton candy, chock-full of artificial flavors and colors.

Part Two. Hannah and I took her to the park playground. Wynter made a beeline for the sandbox, where she snatched other kids' toys and held them for ransom. After a while, she got bored. So she started pouring sand on smaller kids. We tried to make her stop, but she said, "It's my choice."

(Laurie has it wrong. Wynter doesn't need to worry about bullies. The bullies are all terrified of Wynter.)

We bribed her away from the playground with a hot pretzel from a cart.

Part Three. Wynter refused to eat the

healthy wheat-free lunch with its wholesome snack of roasted soy nuts that her mother had packed. With our own money, we bought her a hot dog on a roll, an orange pop, and an ice cream. She wolfed them down.

Part Four. A completely exhausted Hannah and I took Wynter back to my house.

Wynter whined the whole way home. She threatened to wet her pants. We promised her a chocolate bar if she waited just a few more minutes. We ran the last three blocks and got home in the nick of time. After she went to the bathroom we handed her the chocolate and put her in front of the television. She chose to watch a program about a family of singing aardvarks.

Hannah and I watched it with her

Part Five. Laurie came home two hours later. We were still watching singing aardvarks. (Question: How can any responsible television channel air two and a half straight hours of aardvarks? Don't they have a conscience?)

Laurie kissed Wynter, then flopped down on a chair. "What did you do today?" she asked her daughter.

Hannah and I looked at each other. Once Laurie heard about our day, she'd never ask us to babysit Wynter again. I just hoped that she wouldn't be too nasty about the hot dog, the soda, the pretzel, the cotton candy, the chocolate, the ice cream, and a few other things that I won't even mention.

"We had a fun day!" Wynter said innocently. "We went to the zoo and the park. Hannah and Abby are nice. I like them!"

Wynter started to tell her mother about our exciting, eventful day together. She didn't say a word about all the kids who were going to have nightmares about her tonight. Nor did she say anything about the wheats, sweets, and meats we had bought her.

(Note: Wynter's fibbing is world-class. I may give her a food-stained page in the Hayes Book of World Records.)

I nudged Hannah. "Psst. Why isn't she telling on us?"

"It's the junk food," Hannah whispered. "I think she's hoping to get more."

Part Six. My mother walked into the living room. She was dressed up, like she usually is when she has to appear in court. She wore a raw-silk tailored suit, high heels, and a string of pearls. Mom looked so elegant! I was proud of her.

LANCASTER ELEMENTARY SCHOOL

Fifth-Grade Yearbook

ABBY

HANNAH

CASEY

BETHANY

NATALIE

MASON

BRIANNA

VICTORIA

MS. KANTOR

MS. BUNDER

OUR FIFTH-GRADE STARS

Most Likely to Ride on a Spaceship: Natalie

Purplest Pen Person: Abby

Total Techies: Tyler and Zach

Best Sense of Humor: Abby and Mason

Most Disgusting Sense of Humor: Mason

Most Positive: Hannah

Most Likely to Appear on Silver Screen: Brianna

Fanciest Fans of Fashion: Brianna and Victoria

All-Around Athlete: Casey

Wildest Imagination: Natalie

Most Kind to Animals and Other Living Creatures: Bethany

Most Missed: Jessy (the classmate formerly known as Jessica)

Best Person to Have as a Friend: Abby

Most Likely to Become Demanding Diva: Victoria

CRYSTAL BALL

WHERE WILL WE BE IN 20 YEARS?

Abby: a journalist, writer, or writing teacher like Ms. Bunder

Bethany: will have veterinary clinic, of course

Brianna: an Oscar-winning movie star

Casey: a professional basketball player or high school gym teacher

Hannah: a professional scuba diver, studying tropical fish and living by the ocean

Jessy: a teacher or businesswoman

Mason: a stand-up comedian

Natalie: photographer, mad scientist, or off-Broadway actress

Tyler: computer geek

Victoria: heading her own fashion design company

Zach: designer of computer games

MY FRIENDS

I'M, LIKE, SO TOTALLY FED UP WITH ELEMENTARY SCHOOL. I'M OUT OF HERE!
VICTORIA

Never forget; I'm the best.
Brianna

Hamsters rule! Let's hang out this summer.
Bethany

Sixth grade, Here we come!!! Purple Pens forever!
xoxo Hannah

Mason
Brianna says, and never mind what You're the best, Abby, BURP!!!

H.A.G.S.
(Have A Great Summer), Hayes!
Casey

To a very special student,
"Purple Hayes!"
You were so much fun to have in class.
Great work!
Don't stop writing and stay in touch,
Ms. Bunder

Abby,
I will miss your warm smile and thoughtful comments. Don't lose your enthusiasm for writing!! Fifth grade won't be the same without you.
Take care, Ms. Kantor

Abby,
It was fun passing notes in class with you! Thanks for the great Peter Pan script. I CAN FLY!!!
See you in middle school.
Natalie

YOUR FRIENDS

Even if you're not graduating from fifth grade,
ask your friends to write special messages
to you in the space below.

Cya
Later
Elementory?
Hello Junior
High!
Amanda

High Fives: Our Best Memories from Fifth Grade

Movie Night
(Abby dressed up in honor of the film, *Merlin's Magic School*.)

Fifth-grade play: *Peter Pan*
(starring Natalie)

Science Fair
(Abby and Casey made rocks by blending paper, water, and glue.)

Lancaster Lark, the School Newspaper
(Abby was an advice columnist, "Gabby Abby.")

"The legal eagle in her power suit," Laurie remarked.

Her tone of voice wasn't that nice, but Mom just smiled as if it were a compliment. She kicked off her high heels and sank down on the sofa. "How did the babysitting go, girls?"

I shrugged.

"Fine," Hannah said.

"They did a good job," Laurie said.

Mom looked pleased.

Laurie crossed her legs under her. Her bare feet were dirty. She scratched a mosquito bite on her elbow.

"Abby could watch Wynter every day," she announced.

"Yes?" Mom said.

_No!_ I thought, in horror.

"No one has done this well with Wynter in a long time," Laurie said. "You might not believe it, but we have a hard time finding babysitters who understand Wynter's special needs."

"We're very proud of Abby," Mom agreed. "And Hannah, too, of course."

"But –" I said.

Before I could say anything, Laurie went on. "So Abby will be Wynter's babysitter while we're here."

Wynter took her braid out of her mouth and smiled.

Chapter 12

> **Thursday** afternoon
>
> "Better to accept
> whatever happens."
>
> — *Horace*
>
> **Stoic Calendar**

My mom looked at me with tears in her eyes. (Really.) She said, "You're the best, Abby. You never cease to amaze me."

Then I HAD to accept what had happened. I was Wynter's babysitter.

But what if I hadn't accepted it?

What I Might Have Done Instead

1. Suddenly come down with an extremely contagious illness.

2. Hopped around the room like a chimp.

3. Fainted.

4. Screamed.
5. Foamed at the mouth.
6. Said firmly, "I don't want to."

Oh, never mind!
  I better just accept this. I'll remember my summer motto: take things as they come. Even though it's completely unfair. And Laurie didn't pay me for my work. I wonder if she's planning to pay me at all.

  Hannah said she would help me out. She said she wouldn't desert me in my hour of need. She said it was a dirty trick and she had to rally to my side.
  Even though Wynter is a spoiled, seed-spitting, braid-sucking nightmare and we are spending all of our spare cash on bribing her with junk food, Hannah is still standing by me.
  Hannah is the best friend ever.

When I told them what had happened,
Eva and Isabel were pretty mad, too.
They offered to talk to Mom and "set her
straight."

But I said no.
I don't want to disappoint my mother.
Besides, she thinks Laurie is wonderful.
Why should I spoil the visit?
I just hope that Laurie and Wynter
leave SOON.

On top of everything, we have to go to
Laurie's concert tonight. Mom says we
can't miss it. She said Laurie is brilliant
and that one day we'll brag that she
stayed at our house
(Sure, Mom. Right.)
Alex has a sleepover at camp tonight. So
we offered Hannah his ticket. She's coming
with us. Hooray!

In the backseat of the Hayes van, on the way to Laurie's concert, Abby's head sank slowly onto her chest. She sat up with a jerk, then fell asleep again.

Wynter leaned over and poked her hard. "Wake up!" she ordered.

"Sleep," Abby murmured. She couldn't keep her eyes open. How could Wynter still be awake?

It had been another exhausting day with Wynter. Today, Abby and Hannah had taken her to the pool.

"At least she'll get clean," Abby had whispered to Hannah. "I'd love to see her get out of those disgusting clothes."

"Doesn't her mother make her change them?"

" 'It's Wynter's choice whether or not to wear clean clothes,' " Abby recited. " 'She's learning to make decisions.' "

"Good grief," Hannah said.

For a while, things went well at the pool. Wynter played happily in the water. She splashed a few kids who didn't seem to mind. She tried to doggy paddle. But then she got hungry. She bit a little boy.

"Out!" the lifeguard said.

Abby and Hannah took Wynter home, where she cut up one of the calendars in Abby's collection, spilled juice on the couch, and teased T-Jeff. She also ate a pint of cookie dough ice cream.

It was a day that Abby wanted to forget as soon as possible.

And they still had to attend Laurie's concert.

Is the concert adding injury to insult? Abby wondered. Or insult to injury? Which will be worse, a day with Wynter or an evening as Laurie's captive audience?

Hannah was sitting next to Wynter, who was sticking out her tongue at people in other cars. Abby was on Hannah's other side. Eva and Isabel were in the seat in front of them, hooked up to portable CD players. Their parents were in front.

The van stopped abruptly at a red light.

"Almost there," Paul called.

"Abby, I have to tell you what my dad did," Hannah whispered. "I hope you're not upset. I just found out."

"What?" Abby said.

Hannah took a deep breath. "He bought really cheap airline tickets on the Internet today. We're going on a last-minute vacation."

"You are?" Abby gasped. Suddenly, she was wide awake. "When?"

"Tomorrow," Hannah replied.

"*Tomorrow?*" Abby wailed.

Hannah gave her a sympathetic glance. "You'll be fine without me."

"No, I *won't*!"

Hannah glanced at Wynter and whispered, "Maybe they'll leave after the concert."

"Or maybe I'll be her babysitter for life," Abby said glumly. "A fate worse than death!"

"Who's dead?" Wynter looked over at her.

"No one." Abby stared out the window. She wished that she could disappear into the darkness.

As they walked up the stairs to the club, Abby was quiet. Hannah was telling everyone about her family's last-minute vacation. "It was all done on the Internet," she explained.

"Sounds great," Eva said. "Why don't *we* do that, Mom?"

"YES!" Abby shouted. An impromptu trip was the answer to all of her problems. They'd get away from Laurie and have a vacation, too.

"With our crazy schedules? We'd have to plan a last-minute escape twenty years in advance!" Olivia said.

Abby sighed deeply. *Not* having a schedule wasn't that much fun, either. It could be positively dangerous, especially with Laurie and Wynter around.

"Doesn't look like much," Paul said as they entered the Driftwood Club.

A few old posters were tacked on the walls. At one end was a pool table. A piano and a microphone stood forlornly by themselves. A couple of amplifiers were plugged into the walls.

Isabel yawned. "How long is this going to be?"

"Laurie," Wynter whined. "Laurie, Laurie, Laurie . . ."

"This better be good," Paul said.

"Wait until you hear her," Olivia promised her family. "It'll be worth your while." She led them to an empty table.

The room grew more crowded. A man sat down at the piano and played a few introductory chords.

There was a sudden stir as Laurie emerged.

Wynter waved wildly at her mother, who didn't seem to see her.

Laurie was wearing a long black strapless dress, and her hair was down. Her lips were deep red and her eyes were made-up. She didn't look like an ordinary person anymore. She looked like a superstar!

Chapter 13

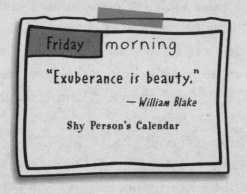

Friday morning

"Exuberance is beauty."
— William Blake

Shy Person's Calendar

Onstage, Laurie was a COMPLETELY different person. She was happy. She was
alive. She was laughing. She was beautiful.
She was exuberant.

Exuberance means liveliness. When she was
performing, Laurie was very lively!

Laurie performed jazz and pop tunes. She
put on a great show.

We were all completely surprised. (Except
maybe Wynter. She fell asleep with her
head on the table. I almost felt sorry for
her.)

* * *

Mom said "I told you so" about a million times.

Best Moment of Evening: Laurie dedicated a song to her "old college roommate and friend, Livy Hayes." The song was called "The Way We Were."

Laurie did another show at midnight. We didn't stay. We all went home to sleep.

After everyone was in bed, I heard Dad say to Mom, "Okay, she's a good singer, but she's still loony!"
Then I fell asleep.

I'm glad I saw the show last night. Now I know why Mom likes Laurie, even if she's kind of awful sometimes.
But I hope I don't have to watch Wynter today. Especially without Hannah here to help me.

When Abby went to hang her wet bathing suit and towel on the clothesline Friday morning, Laurie and

Wynter were sitting at the picnic table having breakfast.

In jeans and an old T-shirt, without makeup, Laurie looked like an ordinary person drinking a cup of coffee. But some of last night's glamour still clung to her. Abby could imagine her in that long gown, singing in front of the crowd.

"I liked your singing," Abby said shyly.

"The late show was even better," Laurie said. "I brought the house down." She took a sip of her coffee. "Did you notice that the pianist couldn't keep up with me during the first few songs?"

"I didn't notice." Abby shook out her wet towel and clipped it to the clothesline.

Laurie smiled. "The club manager said it was one of the best shows they've had this year. My European tour is really going to be something."

Wynter stared at Abby's wet hair. "I want to go swimming with you, Abby."

"Um, maybe."

"Wynter, we're going to the movies," Laurie said. "Remember? If Abby's free, she can join us."

"I have plans," Abby said quickly. Hannah was gone, but Casey might be home. Or maybe she'd go to the library for the afternoon. How wonderful to have time to herself. This was how all her time was supposed to be!

"Have fun," Laurie said. She pulled a wad of bills from her purse and began to count them. There were twenties, fifties, and even a few hundred-dollar bills. "I made a pile of money last night," she bragged.

Abby wondered if Laurie would offer her ten or twenty dollars for babysitting. That would be nice. It would pay for all the treats that she and Hannah had bought for Wynter, as well as admission to the zoo and the pool.

Laurie folded the money carefully and put it away in her jeans pocket. "The club manager asked me to stay for another few weeks."

"*Here?*" Abby squeaked. "*Now?*"

"Of course," Laurie said. "Livy is delighted."

Chapter 14

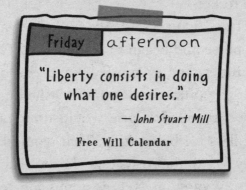

Friday afternoon

"Liberty consists in doing
what one desires."

— John Stuart Mill

Free Will Calendar

I have *NO* liberty.

My summer of post-fifth-grade freedom
has become a summer of servitude!

Note: I just found the word "servitude"
in the dictionary. It means slavery. That
sums it up. I am Laurie's slave for the
summer.

Laurie told Mom that she needed me to
watch Wynter "only a few hours a day."
Mom thinks it's a great idea.

<u>Reasons I Do **NOT** Want the Job</u>
<u>of Babysitting Wynter for a Few</u>
<u>Hours Every Day</u>

1. Laurie never gives me a cent.
2. I am using up all my money on admission fees and snacks for Wynter.
3. Wynter refuses to do anything unless I bribe her with junk food.
4. Wynter lies to her mother about what she eats and does. (Should I tell the truth? Laurie would be furious!)

Help! Help! Help!

<u>Saturday</u>

Mom and Dad had an argument while Laurie and Wynter were out early this morning.

Dad is getting fed up with Laurie. He says he's sick of vacuuming up tiny seeds all over the house and listening to her opinions about the digestive tract. He says she's overstayed her welcome, and he wants her to leave soon. (YAY, DAD!)

Mom defended Laurie. She likes

having her college friend around the house. She said, "It's just like the good old days."

"Maybe the old days weren't as good as you think," Dad answered.

Mom got angry. She said it's her house, too, and she has a right to entertain her friends. She said Dad ought to learn to be more tolerant.

Dad said Mom ought to learn to be more sensitive to the needs of her family.

It's the weekend. Everyone has fun, relaxing plans.

Alex has two days of play dates scheduled.

Eva and Isabel are camping at a state park with their friends.

Dad is participating in a bike marathon.

Mom is golfing in a charity match.

WHAT ABOUT ME?

<u>Sunday Evening</u>
Eva and Isabel returned late from their

camping trip. They had a great time
hiking, canoeing, swimming, and sleeping
under the stars.

Alex watched movies with his
friends, attended a birthday party,
played baseball in the park, and went out
for pizza.

Mom helped raise thousands of dollars for sick children while golfing with
her law partners.

Dad biked for twenty miles yesterday
and came home tanned and relaxed.

I spent "a few hours" with Wynter.
Ha! It was **NINE HOURS, SIXTEEN
MINUTES, TWENTY-THREE SECONDS**.
Don't I get weekends off?

Monday
Dad holed up in his office. Tries not to
come out when Mom and Laurie are together. Has declared strike as family cook.

Hayes family reduced to diet of frozen
pizza, macaroni and cheese from a box, and
grilled cheese sandwiches.

Laurie makes sarcastic remarks about Mom's "gourmet" cooking and lectures us on fat content and toxic chemicals while eating almonds and papaya spears.

Wynter lies on floor and spits out whole-grain rice cereal.

Tuesday
Babysitting Wynter. Guess how long? Guess how much?

Funds almost gone. Can't afford to bribe Wynter with junk food much longer.

Dad seems to have disappeared. Is he alive?

Wednesday
Too depressed to write.

Thursday
I CAN'T TAKE IT ANYMORE!

Chapter 15

Friday

"After three days, fish and guests begin to stink."

Happy Hostess Calendar

Laurie and Wynter have been here a LOT longer than three days! (And Wynter doesn't change her clothes very often.)

"Where's your father?" Olivia Hayes asked as she came in through the back door, her arms laden with packages.

"Working?" Abby said. She was at the kitchen table with her journal opened in front of her.

Olivia set down the packages. She pushed back a strand of hair from her face. "It's hot outside!" She sighed. "What's Wynter doing? Did you watch her today?"

"*Yes,*" Abby said. "As usual."

"Wait until you find out what real work is like," her mother said. "A couple of hours a day is nothing. Besides, it's a favor for an old friend."

"She's not *my* old friend," Abby replied. "And it's definitely *not* a couple of hours a day."

Olivia interrupted her. "I thought you felt okay about doing this, Abby."

"Mom, listen to me . . ." Abby began.

Her voice trailed off as her father came into the kitchen.

"There you are, Paul," Olivia said. "Will you unload the charcoal from the van?"

"Sure," he said. He disappeared out the door, and in a moment reappeared with two huge bags of charcoal. "Back porch?" he asked.

"Thanks," his wife said. "Next to the grill."

"Let's have a barbecue this weekend," he said after depositing the bags on the porch floor.

"Sounds great," Olivia said. "Are you the cook again?"

Paul ran his fingers through his hair and sighed. "If Laurie doesn't check the pedigree of the chicken."

Olivia smiled. "It *is* a bit much, isn't it?"

"I just wish she'd relax," Paul said. "I don't mind

what she eats if she stops lecturing me on what *I* eat."

"Are all those artificial things really bad for you?" Abby asked.

"Some of them are," her father admitted. "But our diet is mostly healthy. A little junk food once in a while is okay."

"*Good,*" Abby said.

"Don't worry, Abby. You can eat your Tooty Frooty cereal," her mother said. "Don't take Laurie too seriously."

"Yes, but — " Abby began again.

"Livy!" Laurie hurried into the kitchen. She looked upset. "You won't believe what I found in Wynter's sleeping bag!"

"Soy nuts?" Paul murmured. "Garlic sesame bars?"

"I found *chocolate*!"

"Oh, dear," Olivia said. "Did Wynter sneak into Paul's office? He keeps a secret stash of chocolate bars there," she explained to Laurie.

"Wynter would never *sneak*," Laurie said. "She respects others' property."

"Anyway, Abby and I ate the last of my supplies a few days ago," Paul said with a laugh.

"This is no laughing matter," Laurie snapped.

"A few pieces of chocolate won't hurt anyone," Olivia said.

"That's not true," Laurie said. "Wynter has a very delicate digestive system."

"Of course," Olivia said soothingly.

"Someone's been giving it to her deliberately," Laurie said. "I want to know who."

"Maybe she found it," Paul suggested. "Or bought it in a store."

"Impossible." Laurie looked hard at Abby.

Abby's heart pounded. She felt heat rising into her face.

"Is it *you*?" Laurie asked.

Abby looked back at her. She took a breath. "Yes," she said. "It is. It was my choice."

Now I know what the expression "the earth stood still" means.

The earth stood still as my mother and father turned to look at me. My mother seemed angry, and my father seemed like he was trying not to smile.

Laurie seemed shocked, as if she hadn't expected me to admit it.

Then she began talking very fast and very loud.

At this point, the earth stopped standing still. It began whirling wildly around me. I felt like I was on one of those crazy rides at an amusement park. I could barely take in a word Laurie was saying.

My mother motioned for Laurie to be quiet, but she wouldn't stop. She said I had betrayed an innocent child's trust. She said Wynter would bear lifelong scars. She made it sound like I had committed an awful crime.

"Enough," Dad said. "Let's calm down and get this in perspective. We're talking about a few pieces of chocolate here."

"Abby deliberately gave Wynter sugar. She knows how bad it is for her."

"It's true," I admitted.

"What are you going to do about this, Paul and Livy?" Laurie demanded. "She's your daughter!"

"In this house, we don't mete out life sentences in prison without a trial." Mom laughed at her own joke. "Abby, we need to hear from you. What's your side of the story?"

I took another deep breath. Then I said everything that was on my mind.

"I've used twenty-three dollars of my own money and seven dollars of Hannah's to buy treats for Wynter," I said. "That's because she won't cooperate unless I bribe her. She sits down and refuses to move unless I buy her candy or ice cream. Sometimes she threatens to wet her pants."

"That's a lie!" Laurie said.

I continued. "She won't listen to anything I say unless I give her junk food. I watch her for eight to nine hours a day. It's been nine days. Laurie hasn't paid me a cent." I counted on my fingers. "That's at least seventy-five hours of unpaid la-bor."

"Unpaid?" Mom said. "I'm <u>sure</u> Laurie intends to pay you . . ."

"Oh, no, I don't!" Laurie cried.

This time my parents looked really shocked.

"You've been leaving Wynter with Abby for eight or nine hours a day? And not paying her?" Mom said to Laurie. "This is not acceptable."

"She didn't take good care of Wynter," Laurie replied.

Mom looked furious. "You lied to me, and you took advantage of Abby. And Wynter sounds like a very difficult little girl."

"I ought to report your daughter," said Laurie.

"Have you ever heard of child labor laws?" Mom said coldly.

Laurie glared at Mom. Her face was red "I thought you were my friend, Livy," she finally said. "But I should have known better."

Chapter 16

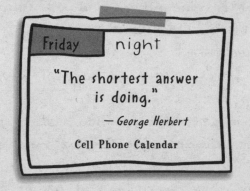

Friday night

"The shortest answer
is doing."

— George Herbert

Cell Phone Calendar

Mom did it.

When Laurie stomped out of the Kitchen,
Mom followed her upstairs. We could all
hear their raised voices.

And then, a miracle happened.

Laurie and Wynter left our house.
In less than half an hour, they
packed their things and drove away —
without saying good-bye or thank you.

When Mom came back downstairs, Dad
didn't say anything. He just put his arm
around Mom's shoulder.

A little while later, Mom handed me an envelope.

Inside was two hundred and seventy-five dollars! In cash!

I gasped. "For me?"

"It's wages and reimbursement of miscellaneous expenses," Mom said.  "Paid by Laurie for your excellent care of her impossible child."

"I gave Wynter a <u>lot</u> of junk food," I admitted.

"Good," Mom said. "It's healthy for her."

I stared at my mother in amazement. "How did you get Laurie to pay me?"

She shook her head and smiled. And she didn't say another word.

"Spill it, Abby," Eva said.

The three Hayes sisters were cleaning up the guest room.

"We want to hear the gory details of what it was like to watch Wynter," Isabel said, stripping dirty sheets from the bed.

"And what Mom said to Laurie," Eva added. "Tell us about their fight."

"It's a really long story," Abby warned. She picked up a rag and began dusting the bureau.

"We want every word," Isabel said.

"Okay," Abby said.

"What a terror!" Isabel cried as Abby told about Wynter at the zoo, Wynter at the pool, Wynter at the playground, and Wynter at the Hayes house. "I had no idea she was *that* bad."

"I don't know what I would have done," Eva said. She put a bouquet of wilted flowers outside the door. "The singing aardvarks alone would have tipped me over the edge."

"And Laurie tricked you into it, too." Isabel shook her head. "I didn't know that adults could be that nasty."

"Laurie is *not* a nice person," Abby said. But as she said it, she remembered Laurie on the night she sang. She had been a completely different person then. Which was the real Laurie?

"Thank goodness she's gone!" Isabel said.

"I still can't believe it's over," Abby said. "I

keep thinking they're going to walk through the door."

"If they do, we'll throw them out again," Isabel promised.

"I guess I can relax," Abby said. "It's going to take a few days."

"You have five more weeks until sixth grade starts," Eva said.

"No!" Abby cried. "I don't want to think about middle school!"

"Are you *nervous*, Abby?" Eva demanded. "After Wynter, middle school is going to be easy."

"Nothing's going to be hard from now on," Isabel said. "Wynter is a tougher customer than anything you'll encounter in middle school."

"Are you sure?" Abby asked.

"*We're sure*," Eva and Isabel said together.

Isabel shook out a blanket and folded it. "So, Abby, do you have plans for the money Mom extracted from Laurie?" She lowered her voice. "Mom told me that Laurie threw the money at her. Right in front of Wynter."

"Wow," Eva said. "That's pathetic."

"But she was a great singer," Abby reminded her

sisters. Then she thought for a moment. "I'm going to give some of the money to Hannah. And maybe I'll buy a new outfit for the first day of school, or get a haircut. Or buy jewelry or a new purse."

"The new, improved Abby Hayes!" Isabel cried. "Going to sixth grade!"

"Yeah. Something like that." Abby's face got hot. "I mean, I'm not turning into Brianna."

"Of course not," Eva said. "But it's good to have a new look for middle school. It's the perfect time to remake yourself." She got down on her hands and knees. "There are sunflower seeds and raisins everywhere! What did they do, throw them around the room like confetti?"

"This sleeping bag has to be disinfected," Isabel said briskly. "It smells awful."

"I'm done dusting," Abby said. "What else should I do?"

"Go relax," Eva said.

Abby slipped quietly out of the room. She was going to tell T-Jeff that it was now safe to come out from under the bed.

THE END (almost)

"Attention! Attention!" Paul Hayes called. "Announcing a special Hayes family event! To celebrate Laurie's departure, we're having a fast-food feast."

An excited buzz spread through the house.

"Hamburgers!" Eva cried. "With everything on them."

"Hot dogs with mustard and pickles!" Alex said.

"I want french fries and ketchup," Isabel said. "And onion rings and those hot apple pastries."

"I think I'll have a milk shake," Abby said. "One of those frothy vanilla ones."

"You're going to make yourselves sick," Olivia scolded. "I'm having some delicious soy yogurt with roasted pumpkin seeds for dinner!"

"*MOM!*" All four of the Hayes siblings yelled at once.

Olivia grinned. "Fooled you," she said.

THE END